Commander You You
and the
Imperial Diamond

Commander You You
and the
Imperial Diamond

Lauren-Kate Stewart

The Bridge
Huntersville, NC

ISBN-13: 9780615918761

Produced in the United States of America

The Bridge
Huntersville, NC
thebridgemedium@gmail.com

For Abby and David
and
my writing group

Contents:

Acknowledgments

Prologue

The Beginning

Commander You You was kidnapped when she was four and was taken to a planet called Yinksa. She never really knew her parents. Commander You You escaped when she was eight and went to an island that was floating in space. There she found another girl just like herself who had been kidnapped and had also escaped. Her name was Abby, and she was 4 feet tall with brown hair and green eyes. Commander You You was also 4 feet tall but had blond hair and blue eyes.

Commander You You had forgotten the name that she had been given by her parents in the four years that she was a prisoner on the Planet Yinksa. So Abby started calling her Commander You You. She got the name Commander You You because she was always calm and creative, she took initiative and she was usually the leader. The people on the planet Yinksa had always called her "little girl," but she did not like that name. So she changed it to Commander You You.

As the years went by Commander You You and Abby began to explore the island. In their expeditions into the woods they found monkeys, snakes, lizards, toads, frogs and turtles. On one of these expeditions they found a large house which had evidently been abandoned by someone who had previously lived on the island. They decided to clean it up and make it into their house. As they were cleaning, snakes and other animals that had been living in the leaves that had fallen into the house through the small gaps in the roof scurried out and went back to live in the woods.

In one corner, however, the girls noticed a small golden ball that was curled up. When Abby picked it up, it uncurled itself, and they saw that it was a small, fluffy, baby kitten. They decided to keep and take care of him; and because he was so fluffy and cute they named him Fluffy.

One day when Commander You You and Abby were outside, a spaceship flew down and landed on the roof of the house. The man in the spaceship was very kind. He asked questions about how they had gotten there and where their parents were. After they told him he seemed satisfied with their answers. He said that he just wandered around in his spaceship getting food and anything else he needed from the nearby planets.

Offhandedly, he said he had enough money to buy another spaceship. He told them that if they helped him restock his food supply, he would give them his current space ship. The girls agreed to this. They went off through the woods with him to find bananas, guavas, pineapples and other fruits, vegetables and meat. After doing this they made their way back to the spaceship. He unloaded his possessions from his own spaceship and put them into the tow ship that was behind his own ship.

After the man left, Commander You You and Abby immediately began to explore in their new spaceship.

This story begins when Commander You You and Abby are 10 years old, know the island well and have many pets.

Chapter 1

An Odd Trip
to the Grocery Store

Commander You You and her friend, Abby, lived on an island covered in trees. In the middle of the island was a large house where Commander You You and Abby lived with their cat, Fluffy. They had many other pets, including a 20-foot-long python, several monkeys and many lizards.

One day, Commander You You announced, "I'm going to the grocery store on the planet FinclBincl to get snake food and to restock our space cereal."

"All right," said Abby. "I will stay here and look after the new, brown, baby monkey."

On her way to the grocery store, Commander You You was surprised to see one of His Imperial Overcookedness's (HIOC) ships hovering off the planet Linkalonk.

Now, everyone knew about HIOC. He was the king of a planet made entirely out of pasta, pasta sauce and metal. All the people were made of pasta and all the liquids were sauce. Everything else was made out of metal. Everyone knew that HIOC was plotting to take over the entire universe, but they didn't see how he could do it with an army of pasta. Even Commander You You and Abby had heard about HIOC on their many visits to the planet FinclBincl.

Commander You You was astonished to see HIOC loading something large and white into his ship.

Now, as you can imagine, there are not many large, white, and sparkly objects in space. When Commander You You used her binoculars, she was stunned to see that the object was the famous Imperial Diamond of which all had heard. It belonged to King Ufa Gufa, King of the planet Linkalonk.

Just at that moment HIOC's ship took off.

Commander You You knew that her ship was too slow and bulky to follow HIOC's sleek and fast ship and see where it went. She did not know if HIOC or any of the men on his ship had seen her, so, as a precaution, she went back to her island to pick up Abby before warning King Ufa Gufa.

When Commander You You got home she went immediately to find Abby.

"Abby," Commander You You called.

"Over here."

Commander You You found Abby trying to keep the tiny baby monkey from pushing over the table that was in front of the pantry. If the monkey managed to get into the pantry by pushing over the table, he and his friends would probably eat all the food or throw it around.

Abby looked up when she saw Commander You You and quickly stopped laughing when she saw the serious expression on her friend's face.

"Abby, HIOC has stolen the Imperial Diamond! I saw him do it! As you know, whoever has the Imperial Diamond can rule the universe. We have to go warn King Ufa Gufa, or HIOC will take over the galaxy!"

Chapter 2

Commander You You and Abby Become Part of King Ufa Gufa's Secret Army

Abby and Commander You You put Fluffy into his cat carrier. The girls gathered some food, got into their spaceship and traveled to the planet Linkalonk to warn King Ufa Gufa of the impending disaster.

When they got an audience with the king, Commander You You explained what she had seen that morning.

"Your information is good but not

surprising," said the king. "I knew that the Imperial Diamond had been stolen, for HIOC took it right out of my bare hands! He went up to his ugly bathtub of a ship and went off to that mushy Pasta Planet or whatever it's called."

"Unfortunately," he continued, "all the soldiers who could get it back for me are off fighting a war against King Yagaflag and his entire planet of Grompleygook." (King Yagaflag had insulted King Ufa Gufa most severely. Without the Imperial Diamond, King Ufa Gufa's army was not unbeatable.)

"That is serious, indeed!" said Abby and Commander You You.

Fluffy whined in his cat carrier and scratched the edge.

"Your Chihuahua wants a treat," said King Ufa Gufa.

"He's not a Chihuahua. He's a cat!" the girls said indignantly. And Fluffy meowed in reproach.

"Sure looks like a Chihuahua to me," said the king. "Chihuahua or no Chihuahua, we have to find someone who can get back the Imperial Diamond. I know just the people! Since I don't have any of my regular spies, or soldiers, or, you know, people who do stuff for me, you two will go and get the

Imperial Diamond for me. Oh, and take your Chihuahua with you."

"Us??? But we're only 10 years old!" said Commander You You.

"Exactly! That's why I chose you two."

"What? But we have animals, and a home, and stuff! Why would we go get the Imperial Diamond for you? Why wouldn't you send one of your servants or something?"

"I can't send any of the servants, because they are, well, too big. And I don't really have anyone else. I mean, I can't let my nine-year-old nephew, David, go and get it."

"Why not?" the girls both said in unison.

"Because he's my nephew and the heir to my throne, of course!"

"Oh... well, that explains it," said Abby sarcastically.

"You will go and get the diamond back for me!" said King Ufa Gufa haughtily. "By royal decree. I order you to go and get the Imperial Diamond!"

"But we're only kids!" they said in protest again.

"That doesn't matter. You can slip by HIOC easier and faster than adults can. So, I royally command you to go and get the Imperial Diamond!"

"Well, I guess we can't say anything against a 'royal decree,'" said Commander You You.

"Exactly! You can't do anything against a royal decree. So, you must pick out one of my spaceships and go and get the Imperial Diamond now," said King Ufa Gufa imperiously.

Commander You You and Abby were very worried they might never see their home again. They were afraid they might get captured by HIOC and be stuck in one of his dungeons forever. But they knew that they could not go against the royal decree of King Ufa Gufa.

Just as they were about to leave, King Ufa Gufa said that they must return the Imperial Diamond in five days.

"As both of you know, the power of the Imperial Diamond lets the person who possesses it rule the entire galaxy. His armies will be unstoppable, and no country will dare invade his planet."

"But that means HIOC will be unstoppable!" Abby and Commander You You cried in dismay.

"Exactly! That's why you must stop him before he gains the full power of the Imperial Diamond."

"And how long will that take him?" Abby and Commander You You inquired.

"Five days," said King Ufa Gufa gravely.

"Five days! How are we supposed to stop him in that amount of time?"

"Sneak into his palace and take the Imperial Diamond," said King Ufa Gufa as though it would be the easiest thing in the world to waltz into the palace and take back the diamond.

"As you may well know," the king said, "the Imperial Diamond has been handed down in my family for generations. My family, of course, has always used it for the good of the people and never for any evil purposes. But HIOC is different. He will use it for his own evil ends and will try his best to take over the universe."

"I hate having deadlines!" said Abby.

"And especially such an important one!" said Commander You You.

"Yes, it is most important. Remember, we must have the Imperial Diamond out of the hands of HIOC in five days; otherwise, HIOC will take over the universe."

"One minor point. Why haven't you yourself taken the step to rule over the entire universe?" Commander You You asked King Ufa Gufa.

"Because, I am, well,…I don't particularly want to rule the entire universe. If I were to rule the entire universe, then, that would mean I would have the entire universe and no one left to conquer. And, even more, I'm happy ruling my little kingdom, with my people, and I think my people like me, and I'm happy that way. I don't want to rule a huge kingdom. Ruling a huge kingdom is good, but it's bad. I am perfectly happy ruling my own little kingdom."

"Well, anyhow, you had better get on your way," King Ufa Gufa said, realizing that he had been talking for quite some time. "You'd better get going to the spaceships so I can have my Imperial Diamond back. Oh, and one more thing to remember, HIOC is not going to be nice to you if you get caught. So, don't get caught. And above all other things, don't let him know that I sent you. He'll make war on me. And I certainly don't want a war with him."

"You'd better go and look at my spaceships and pick one to take. It should be small and stealthy."

Taking these important instructions, Abby and Commander You You went down a passage that led to the spaceships.

When they were looking at them, suddenly there was a thunderous crash followed immediately by a loud meow.

"What was that?" said Abby in surprise and alarm.

"And where is Fluffy?" said Commander You You.

They rushed over to the spot where the noise came from and found Fluffy in the middle of a destroyed spaceship. Commander You You picked up Fluffy who was not hurt, only startled.

"Fluffy you should know better than to wander off," Commander You You said when they had gone back to looking for a spaceship. Fluffy looked at Commander You You and Abby apologetically.

"Wait a second. This one is perfect for us," said Commander You You.

The ship was dark colored with small clear windows that would let them see out. It looked fast, and they thought it might be able to outrun one of HIOC's ships.

"Come on, guys. Let's go!" said Commander You You.

Just then, King Ufa Gufa came storming in. He glared menacingly. In an extremely angry voice he said, "Who destroyed my favorite spaceship?"

"Come on!" Abby exclaimed. "Let's get out of here!"

"Come back here, you ship destroyers!" King Ufa Gufa cried.

Fluffy ran toward the ship and darted in. Abby and Commander You You followed quickly slamming the door behind them. The girls started the engine and took off, to find HIOC and the Imperial Diamond.

Chapter 3

Commander You You and Abby Get Caught by a Bunch of Dinner Food

"Phew! That was close! We almost got thrown into the dungeon."

"Yeah, I'm glad that's over," Abby sighed in relief.

"Hey! What's that little speck? Is it a planet?"

"I don't think so," said Abby. "It's too shiny to be a planet."

As the thing got closer they saw that it was a ship.

"Quick! Use the binoculars to see what nationality it is!"

"It's a Pasta Planet ship!" cried Abby "Should we fire?"

"No, wait," said Commander You You. "I don't think the ship has seen us yet. If we get behind that asteroid, we might be able to follow it without them knowing it."

"Do you think?" said Abby.

"Well, it might work, and it's better than standing out here where they could see us," replied Commander You You.

"I hadn't thought of that," said Abby. "I didn't think they'd have binoculars on board their ship. We'd better get behind that asteroid."

They snuck along behind the asteroid until suddenly the ship stopped and began to descend. The Pasta Planet came into view.

There were metal buildings, and some had swimming pools of sauce, and there was one very large building. That was HIOC's royal palace.

"Wow! Look at all that pasta!"

"Yeah, that could last us our whole lives," said Commander You You.

"Where do you think we should land? Do you think we could land on the roof of the royal palace?"

It's worth a shot. Let's go," said Commander You You.

So they went boldly forward and landed on the palace. Just as they were about to exit they heard a shout and several guards ran forward.

"What are you doing here?" the guards asked suspiciously.

"Oh, nothing, we just wanted to pay tribute to HIOC. See, we brought these delicious fruits for him," said Commander You You and Abby. They held up several large, fruit-shaped paint balls.

"You want to taste one?" they said.

"Oh no! It would not be right for me to taste HIOC's royal tributes," the guard said in a tone of horror.

"Well, you're going to taste it anyway, whether you like it or not," said Commander You You and Abby in unison.

With a slight laugh, they threw their fruit-shaped paint balls at the guards, and the startled guards went skidding across the roof. Fluffy meowed tauntingly and ran to join his masters.

"There you go. Bring that to HIOC," cried Abby.

"Come on. Let's go through that little door and see if we can find the Imperial

Diamond," said Commander You You.

"Come back here, you traitors!" shouted the guards.

"Come on. We've got to hurry!" said Abby.

With Fluffy they dashed through the little door, locking it securely behind them. They heard the guards banging outside, trying to get in, and they ran down the first passage they saw. The girls could hear other guards starting to follow them. They worried they would never see their home again and would probably become servants in the palace of HIOC. Gradually, the sounds of shouting guards and tramping feet got louder and louder.

"What are we going to do?" Abby gasped between breaths. "They'll catch us before long! Hey, what's that little sparkly thing in the distance? Do you think it might be the diamond?"

"Come on! Let's find out! And, quickly, before the guards catch us!"

As they got closer, they saw that indeed it was the Imperial Diamond. They could tell because of its size. It was as big as one of their heads. Also, it didn't look like a regular-cut diamond. It looked like someone had just found it in the ground and not bothered to get it cut. The diamond sparkled in the light that was coming down from several lamps above.

"Wait a second. Don't you think that this is too easy?" Commander You You said warily.

"Yeah. Shouldn't there be like top security laser beams or something and lots of guards around it?" said Abby.

"It might be a trap," suggested Commander You You.

Just then a little siren went off, and what Commander You You had said about a trap was quickly verified. Guards came from all sides and they had nowhere to run. The Imperial Diamond started to fade, and the girls realized it was just an image and the real Imperial Diamond must be somewhere else.

Chapter 4

Commander You You and Abby Accidentally Blow up Part of HIOC's Palace

Commander You You and Abby could not see above the heads of their tall pasta guards. But they didn't have to be able to see above their guards to know what was coming. Commander You You and Abby heard the blowing of trumpets and the beating of drums.

The guards parted and a great procession came into view. There were trumpeters, soldiers and every kind of instrument you might have in a band with horses and chariots and, eventually, a gigantic throne on wheels. The throne was all different colors: red, yellow, blue, black, white, gold, silver and purple. It was being pushed by many servants, and Commander You You and Abby both wondered how the throne could support HIOC because he was so fat. He was wearing about as many clothes as someone might wear in three days all on top of each other. They never knew that HIOC was so fat. For indeed, he was extremely fat. They thought the throne might collapse under him.

"Who are you? And why are you in my palace?" boomed HIOC angrily.

"Excuse me, but we are here to take back the Imperial Diamond," Commander You You said.

"What? How do you know the Imperial Diamond is here?"

"Because I saw you steal it."

"That wasn't me.... That was uhhhhh.... All right, fine, it was me."

"If you don't let us go then we'll ummmmm…. Fluffy will scratch you."

"Ha ha ha. Do you think I'm scared by a threat like that?"

"Well... not really, but it was the only thing we had to say," explained Commander You You. "I hope that you're good with cats because Fluffy really really is not in a good mood."

Fluffy's hair rose, and he arched his back and hissed. Suddenly, Fluffy jumped forward and scratched HIOC on the nose.

"How dare you scratch me! Take them to the dungeon!"

"Uh oh. We're in big, big trouble," Abby exclaimed.

"We've been in big, big trouble for a long time now, and I don't think this is any worse than what would have happened if Fluffy hadn't scratched him," said Commander You You philosophically.

Commander You You and Abby were shoved roughly down endless corridors, and they gradually became aware that they were descending. Eventually they came to a door which was securely locked and barred. The guard took out a large key ring and unlocked the many locks and pushed them in, closing the door securely behind them, locking and barring it again.

The dungeon was extremely dark, hot and mildewy. The girls searched all around the edge of the dungeon, but could find no exits.

Eventually, they gave up searching and sat down to rest. Commander You You looked at her watch and saw in amazement that it was nine o'clock at night. They had been searching for three hours! The girls decided they would try to find an exit in the morning.

When they woke up, they began to search again. Commander You You and Abby started to think they couldn't get out when they saw a small beam of light. It was coming from the other side of the dungeon. As they got closer they saw it was a tiny door. They noticed, however, that on the other side was a large pool with mad, red piranhas and hungry blue-spotted sharks in it.

"I don't think we can escape that way," said Commander You You in a desperate voice. "Whatever is down there doesn't look at all friendly, and I'm positive it won't help us."

Fluffy turned around and walked purposefully toward the dungeon door.

"Wait! Fluffy where are you going?" Abby exclaimed. "Come on, let's follow him. Maybe he's found a way out."

He was walking decidedly toward the padlocked door again, and they could hear the sound of the guard outside. Fluffy, when he passed, put his paw under the door and scratched him on the foot.

"Youch! What was that?" shouted the guard in surprise.

When he sat down to check his foot, Fluffy put his paw under the door again, and this time scratched him on the arm. When the guard turned on his side to see where he had been scratched the second time, Commander You You swept her hand under the door and grabbed the large ring of keys. They silently unlocked the door, and Fluffy jumped on top of the guard. Because he was made of pasta, he easily snapped under Fluffy's weight.

"Good job Fluffy!" Abby whispered. "Come on, let's get out of here and go back to our planet and our animals! Let's forget about the Imperial Diamond."

"But how will we get to our ship? It's probably heavily guarded."

"So how can we get away?" said Abby in a worried voice. "Or where can we hide?"

"Maybe we could hide somewhere in the palace. Seems pretty big."

"Yes, but how would we get food or water?" Abby worried.

"I thought of that on the way here," said

Commander You You. "I brought some food in my backpack." She opened the backpack and took out three bottles of water, two cans of cat food, two sandwiches, some milk and a few chips with a banana.

"Wow! How did you get all that food before we left?"

"I found it on the ship. And I found something else that might be useful."

She took out a small circle that kind of looked like it had been cut out of a piece of cardboard.

"Okay.... What's that?" said Abby.

Commander You You touched the middle of the circle and several small buttons of all different colors – red, blue, yellow, white, green and many others – opened up from the center. All the small buttons outlined three big ones.

"Wow! How did you do that?" said Abby in amazement.

"I found it in the locker on the ship with the food, and I ran my hand across it and, all of a sudden, the buttons popped up. I'm not sure what it does, but I thought it might be useful so I kept it."

"Do you think it will help us escape?"

"It might," said Commander You You. "Although I think we should first learn what all the buttons do before we start pressing them."

Just then they heard a shout and the tramping of hurried feet.

"They found out we escaped!"

Commander You You and Abby started running in the opposite direction from which the sound was coming. They ran down many long, winding corridors until finally they came to an open door and jumped in. The room was small and circular with a tiny hole for light in the middle of the ceiling. They hid behind the door and watched through the cracks as the guards ran past looking for them.

A couple of guards ran inside the room but failed to look behind the door, so Commander You You and Abby were safe. After all the guards had passed, the girls tiptoed quietly out and went the opposite way the guards had come so as not to run into them again.

"Phew! That was close," whispered Commander You You.

"Let's see if we can find the exit."

"Wait. I think I hear barking. Oh no! Did they send dogs, too?"

The hair on Fluffy's back rose, and he meowed uncomfortably.

"Quick! See if there's any place to hide in that room!" said Abby pointing to a nearby door.

The room was large and triangular with gigantic pasta strainer windows. There was a large bed in the corner with a mattress that looked like it was made out of muffin dough; but they had no time to look at the fantastic scenery.

They darted in and searched for a place to hide. Abby found a large wooden chest which could fit all three of them. They climbed in and lifted the lid a tiny bit so they could see out and waited breathlessly to see if the dogs would find them. As the dogs got closer they became more and more nervous until finally the dogs came into sight. They were gigantic mastiffs held on leashes. Several pasta men were trying to hold them. The mastiffs entered the room and sniffed around. They sniffed at the chest, but didn't try to open it.

"Guess they're not hiding here," said one of the men holding the dogs. "Come on. Let's check some of the other rooms."

Gradually, the men's voices and the dogs' barking faded away and there was silence.

"Do you think they'll find us?" whispered Abby.

"Not likely. If the dogs failed to find us, then the men won't either, since they are not very smart from what I've seen."

"Well, where do we go now? It's not like we can stay in here forever."

"I propose that we sleep here for the night and, in the morning, slip out and see if we can find an exit which is not heavily guarded. We go out, find a place to hide, steal a spaceship and then try again in a few days."

"But we don't have that much time! And if we don't make it, King Ufa Gufa will put us in the dungeon!" said Commmander You You.

"But if we stay here much longer, we'll be captured and we'll be prisoners," Abby argued.

"Or we could go to King Ufa Gufa and absolutely get thrown into the dungeon," Commander You You pointed out. "We must weigh our options. Here are our choices: go back to our planet, go back to King Ufa Gufa, or stay here and maybe get away with the Imperial Diamond."

"All right. Let's have a sandwich for dinner and then get some rest. In the morning, we'll see if we can find the Imperial Diamond," said Abby.

They each ate their sandwiches. Abby had turkey and Commander You You had ham. Fluffy ate some chicken flavored cat food. Afterwards, they curled up in the chest with Fluffy between them and slept.

In the morning, the girls silently climbed out of the chest and began to look for a way out of the room since the guards had closed and locked the door when they left.

"There is no way we can get out of here. Now we're trapped! We've got less than three days left! If we don't get the Imperial Diamond soon the galaxy will be overrun by pasta people," said Commander You You.

"I know. Let's see if those buttons will do anything," said Abby pointing to the device. "It wouldn't hurt to push them. We're already so messed up that things couldn't get any worse if the room blew up."

"All right. Which button should we push?" said Commander You You.

"Let's push the big blue one," said Abby.

As soon as Abby pushed the button a small stream of light came from the other side of the room.

"Whoa! What did that button do?"

"I don't know, but I think it just opened up a door for us to get out."

"Let's check," said Abby.

When they ran over to the little point of light, Abby and Commander You You saw that it was a tiny door. They looked at the small circle of buttons in disbelief. How could it work in His Imperial Overcookedness's palace? They had found it in King Ufa Gufa's ship so it should only be able to work with King Ufa Gufa's stuff.

"Something just occurred to me," said Abby. "Maybe this device was stolen from HIOC's and the guards might have forgotten to take it off the ship. It might help us in finding the Imperial Diamond and getting out of here."

"Now that you mention that, it makes total sense. Because remember, two months ago, King Ufa Gufa raided HIOC's kingdom. He just might have stolen this little control panel that controls all the doors and exits."

"Wow! So now we have a way to get out. But how do we know where the Imperial Diamond might be?"

"The only person who knows is HIOC and some of his closest advisors, and none of them, especially HIOC, would tell us. How can we get the information?"

"I have an idea," said Commander You You. "We could go and see if we could find one of the royal advisor's rooms and take some of his clothes, then go in disguise and ask for the location of the Imperial Diamond. We could tell the guards we've been ordered to put more security around it or something."

"Wait! What's that sound?" Abby whispered.

"I don't hear anything."

"No, no. There is something," Abby insisted.

Then they heard, "SELF DESTRUCT IN 30 SECONDS!"

Abby and Commander You You ran as fast as they could with Fluffy in tow towards the little door. Once through the door, they looked behind them, and all they could see was ashes.

Chapter 5

Commander You You and Abby Find Out How Dumb HIOC Really Is

"That was close! I'll never look at pasta again!" said Abby

"Let's go see if we can find one of the royal officials."

"All right," agreed Abby. "Where do you think you're going Fluffy?"

"Maybe he's found something. Let's check," Commander You You said as Fluffy walked purposely down the hall.

They followed Fluffy down endless corridors until they saw an open door. They crept in and searched in the closet to see if they could find anything in which to disguise themselves.

"I found something. It looks like a noble's attire that will work perfectly," said Abby. "Now, who will go in disguise?"

"I think it should be you because you have such a great dialect."

"All right," said Commander You You a little reluctantly.

So she put on the noble's dress, which did not fit her at all. The dress was too long, and she looked like the skinniest noble there ever was. She looked like she was wearing something from the 1800s, and she hadn't gotten a fitting for it.

"Don't you think he'll notice my face and my hair?" worried Commander You You.

"Well, we can tie your hair up and put the hat on over it. As for your face, you can pull your hat down way over your eyes so no one will notice. There's one more problem," pointed out Abby. "Where in the world is the throne room?"

"Well, I don't know. We'll just have to look for it and find out," said Commander You You.

They started by walking down a few corridors and looking into every room.

"Do you think we should ask one of the servants?" suggested Abby.

"Don't you think it would be a bit strange to ask the servants where the throne room is? We're pretending to be officials. We should know that."

"Right....Maybe we should just keep looking or maybe we should try pressing another button and see if that does anything. I have a crazy idea," said Abby. "Why don't we ask the panel where the throne room is? Maybe it's like one of those GPS kind of things in the spaceship which responds to your voice."

"Let's try it and find out."

They quietly asked the small circle of buttons to tell them where the throne room was. Nothing happened. But moments later a small arrow appeared on its surface pointing left. After they went left, it pointed right. Then it pointed straight and so on until, finally, words appeared on the panel which said: YOU HAVE ARRIVED.

"Okay,... that was weird. I don't know how a cardboard circle could be able to talk to you," said Commander You You incredulously.

"Maybe it's one of HIOC's special inventions I've heard about. Well, anyway, let's see if we can get into the throne room. Fluffy and I will hide by the door and listen to see what's happening in there," said Abby.

"If anything goes wrong and he discovers me, I'll run to the door. When I'm there, we'll both start running for the nearest door in the hall and hide," said Commander You You.

"Sounds like a plan," agreed Abby.

Abby took Fluffy in her arms and hid behind the door while Commander You You boldly entered the throne room.

Commander You You said in her deepest pasta-like voice, "Excuse me, Your Majesty, but you know those two girls who escaped from the prison? They might have discovered the place where the Imperial Diamond is hidden. They are a very crafty bunch. Now, I know even I do not know the location of the Imperial Diamond; but they might have figured it out. So I would like permission to go to the site of the Imperial Diamond, and, with your permission, put higher security on it."

"Yes, this is a grave matter indeed," said HIOC thoughtfully. "If we do catch them we can not let them escape again if they know the site of the Imperial Diamond. Also, they have my royal escape board panel. If they learn how to use it correctly they can learn all the secrets of my palace. Even the way to my treasury!" (HIOC was quite a miser. He trembled at the thought of people being able to get into his treasury.)

"Oh, yes, Your Majesty! That is right!" agreed Commander You You in disguise. "They must not be able to find your treasury. But isn't the Imperial Diamond much more valuable than your treasury?"

"Oh, yes. Much more valuable than my treasury. Yes, of course, I shall tell you where the site of the Imperial Diamond is. Now that you mention it, it has been somewhat annoying to me that no one else knows the secret of where it is."

"I will take good care that no one finds it, Your Majesty."

"Good. Now, the place where the Imperial Diamond is found. I placed it securely on the planet Lava Lot in the center of the largest volcano."

"You mean the one that has the colony of giants in the middle?" said Commander You You in disguise.

"Yes, I do."

"But that one is impossible to get into!"

"Yes, it is if you don't have the help of my secret control panel which King Ufa Gufa foolishly stole from me. Now, since the control panel is gone, there is only one way in – the secret door, at the back of the volcano. You must sneak in through that door, and the Imperial Diamond is in their treasury. I put it there for safe keeping."

"Those guys! They are complete misers. They will never give it back!" said Commander You You in disguise.

"That's why I hid it there! We can sneak in and get the Imperial Diamond, but anyone else who tries to get in, cannot."

"Brilliant! I think that is one of your best plans yet!"

"Yes, I am a rather stunning genius, aren't I?"

"Oh, yes, Your Majesty, you are the greatest genius of all time!"

"But, on the way in to get the Imperial Diamond, you have to go to the very back of the volcano. There you will find a small door. It is locked, but I do have the key to it. Here, just a moment, let me get it."

He disappeared behind the curtain. When he returned, he was holding an extremely large key.

"Take this and unlock the small door. A path from the door leads into the center of the town. You'll have to go through at night when they are all asleep and sneak into the treasury. The only difficult part is that the key to the treasury is locked inside that little panel that King Ufa Gufa stole from me about a month ago."

"I will find a way in," said Commander You You confidently.

"Very good. Now, please leave me alone. I need to ponder the plans for my new and most grand palace."

Commander You You walked quietly to the door, bowed, and exited.

"You were amazing!" said Abby. "Did you get the location?"

"I got more than that. I got the key to the way in. But there is also some bad news. It's on the planet Lava Lot."

"Lava Lot! But that's where the fearsome giants live! No one goes there!"

"It will take almost two whole days to get there by spaceship," Commander You You said. "We'll only have 24 hours to find the Imperial Diamond. But I guess we'll have to do it."

"Somehow, HIOC got in and hid the Imperial Diamond in the giants' treasury."

"Wait! You mean the giants know about this?"

"Yes, they do, and they are complete misers. They will never give it back."

"But, he gave me the key to the back door, and he also said that the key to the treasury is locked inside our little cardboard circle."

"All right, so how do we get to the planet Lava Lot?" said Abby.

"I don't know. We'll have to get a ship and see if we can find a map somewhere to the planet. All I know is it's somewhere north of here, so if we just head north, we're sure to see it."

"Good point. So how do we get a spaceship?"

"We could…steal one of the private ones."

The private spaceships were used like modern day cars. Anyone who could afford a spaceship could buy one. If a person couldn't afford one, he would a hail a taxi spaceship. If he had a spaceship, he would use it to travel to other planets or buy a ticket at one of the ticket offices to get on board one of the faster spaceship jets. Those could take many passengers and would get there in half the time. Almost all of the private spaceships were kept in spaceship garages which adjoined houses.

"Those are not fast enough, and they're too big! We need one that's fast and small. We should probably look in HIOC's spaceship collection."

"All right. Should we try asking the cardboard circle again?"

"Sure. We can try that," said Abby.

Just then, they heard voices inside. Two guards were talking loudly, obviously arguing.

"You were the one who let them escape!" said one voice.

Then another in a deeper voice said, "No, I didn't! You did! You were the one guarding them."

"Please, please. Now that they have escaped, it doesn't matter who let them escape as long as we find them," said a voice which they all recognized as HIOC's.

"Wait. Do I hear something outside?" said the first voice again.

"Well, if you heard something, go and check!" roared HIOC angrily. "I don't like it when the servants overhear things."

"It didn't sound like one of the servants, Your Majesty. It sounded more like....two kids talking."

"Get them then! If they are the ones who escaped, that is excellent for us! If they're not, then still, we captured them!"

Commander You You and Abby began to run toward the nearest door on the other side of the hall.

"Quick! Find any place we can hide!"

They hurriedly looked around the room but all they found was a closet.

"Come on, let's hide in here," said Abby.

Commander You You and Abby ran into the closet with Commander You You carrying Fluffy. They shut the door behind them and hid among the clothes. They quickly found that the closet was extremely large and didn't end where it was supposed to. Eventually, the girls realized that it led into a long metal passageway.

"Wow! Whoever lives in this room is really lucky! They have their own passageway and everything!" exclaimed Abby.

"Let's see what we can find at the end. It won't hurt to look," Commander You You suggested.

They followed the passageway down to a large room with only one exit. There were spaceships of all kinds. Big ones, little ones, fast ones, slow ones, blue ones, purple ones, green ones. You name it, they had it.

"So... that's neat. But,...how do we choose which one? They all look fast," said Commander You You.

"They have tags on them," said Abby. "Look. This one says, 'VERY SLOW.' And this one says, 'MEDIUM.'"

"Oh, I found one which says, 'ONLY FOR EXTREME EMERGENCIES SUCH AS FIRE, EARTHQUAKE, SAUCE FLOOD AND OTHER DISASTERS.' This is the one for us because I think this is an extreme emergency!"

"Okay, let's try that one," Abby assented. "Hopefully, it's fast enough for our purpose."

They boarded the spaceship and wondered how they were going to get the Imperial Diamond.

Chapter 6

Commander You You and Abby Meet Someone That Makes HIOC Look Small

Abby and Commander You You thoroughly explored the ship. It was small but very neat and had everything you could want: a kitchen, a bathroom, two bedrooms and a dining room. There were several portraits of HIOC pinned up on the walls. The kitchen was well stocked with food and the furniture was nice. Not overly fancy, but not poor. This particular spaceship had obviously been one of HIOC "not so special" spaceships.

When they were finished exploring, they talked over the matter of navigating to planet Lava Lot. They decided to go north till the Pasta Planet was out of sight. They would keep going north till they reached the planet Yinksa, which both of them knew well. Then they would head west from Yinksa. They calculated that would get them fairly close to Lava Lot. When they had agreed on this, Abby and Commander You You revved up the engine, sped down the runway and took off to find the Imperial Diamond. They traveled through space for a long time until they saw a moving line in front of them.

"An asteroid belt!" cried Abby. "Uh oh, do you think we can steer around it?"

"We'd lose too much time, and it's too large," said Commander You You. "We've already used up a day traveling. We have to hurry!"

"We'll have to go through it?" said Abby hesitantly.

"I'm afraid so," said Commander You You in a desperate voice.

As they steered toward it, they started to realize how large the belt actually was.

"That thing is gigantic!" said Commander You You in amazement.

As they began to steer through the asteroid belt, they found that it was much harder than they had expected. The asteroids moved much faster than it had looked like they were moving from a distance. The asteroids came so close to the windshield that they could see all the bumps and ridges and holes in the oddly shaped asteroids. Some were very big; some were small; some moved extremely quickly, and some moved sort of slow.

Fluffy was whimpering in a corner of the ship and tried to hide his face with his paws and tail. Abby wanted to go over, scoop him up and hug him, but she knew she could not do that because she was helping Commander You You steer.

As they tried to navigate around the asteroids, they were constantly afraid they would hit one of them. But, eventually, they made it out safely.

"I'm never ever going to try that again," Abby said in relief.

"Me neither," Commander You You agreed.

Just then they saw several ships coming from what looked like a far off planet. The ships were advancing quickly. Commander You You and Abby knew they couldn't run from them.

"Uh oh! These ships better not be from Yinksa!" said Commander You You.

"Do you think they'd recognize us?"

"Probably not. But they might."

"More likely they'll arrest us for trespassing on their land."

"Yeah, do you think that they'd let us go?" said Abby hopefully.

"No, probably not. But I think we could escape. Well, anyway, here they come. We don't have much choice now!" said Commander You You.

The ships drew alongside. There were five of the Yinksa guards outside the door. Commander You You and Abby were ordered to open the door. When they did, the men seized Commander You You and Abby and roughly carried them into the largest of the Yinksa spaceships.

"What are we going to do now?" said Commander You You.

"Well, let's see if they put a guard over us. Wow! Is that the captain of the ship? He is really, really, really fat."

"How dare you call me fat!" roared the commander of the ship angrily. "I am the skinniest man here," he said while shaking his fist vigorously at them.

It was true. Compared to the commander, some of the soldiers aboard the ship were much fatter. They had to be at least 2,000 pounds. Some were larger."

"Do you have a permit?"

"What for?" said Commander You You innocently.

"Don't you know this is restricted land?"

"Actually, no," said Commander You You in fake surprise.

"Well, I arrest you for trespassing on my land."

"We're extremely sorry sir," said Abby apologetically. "We just wanted to come and give you a present. We thought you might want a new, nice spaceship, and we would go away in our tow ship."

"Yes," said Commander You You. "We are very, very sorry, and we would like to repay you as much as we can."

"You cannot repay me for trespassing on my land except by being imprisoned for a lifetime!"

"Not even a nice spaceship sir?"

"Well... maybe. Umm... well..., okay. A nice spaceship."

"Can we just get our backpack out? It just

has a change of clothes and some food."

"Well... I'm in an extremely generous mood today. And I suppose it wouldn't be too much for you to get your worthless stuff. I suppose you can get it."

"Thank you very much, sir!"

The girls boarded their ship again and took out their backpacks. With Fluffy, they got on their tow ship and watched as the five ships, along with their ship, went off toward the far away planet.

"Well, at least we got away from them, and they didn't take us prisoner," said Abby trying to look on the bright side.

"But, where's the control panel? Do they have it now?"

"Nope! I hid it in the backpack before they came close to us," said Abby.

"That was great thinking, Abby! Let's see if we can quickly get across their territory and to Lava Lot before more ships notice us and try and capture us."

They sped across the territory that Yinksa owned. They were quickly out of sight from the small planet when another tiny red speck appeared. The girls knew that it was Lava Lot and the Imperial Diamond was very close. As they drew closer to the planet, they saw that it was much larger than they had imagined. There was one extremely large volcano in the center that they knew from HIOC's description to be the largest volcano on the planet. It did not have any smoke or lava coming out of it which seemed very odd.

"But how do we know which is the back and which is the front?" asked Commander You You.

"I don't know," said Abby. "Maybe if we go all the way around it, we'll find the door. There. I think I see something that looks a lot like a tiny door down on the ground."

"Well, let's land by it and see," said Commander You You.

Chapter 7

Commander You You and Abby
Step Into a World
Where They Are the Smallest

Commander You You and Abby landed about 10 feet away from the little door. Commander You You took the large key that HIOC had given her and unlocked the door.

She had been able to keep the key because she had hidden it. The people from Yinksa hadn't noticed the large key shaped bulge in her backpack.

"Come on. Let's get inside," said Commander You You.

Abby picked up Fluffy, and they both walked down the dark tunnel. The passage was wet and smelled of mildew like it had not been used in a very, very, very, very long time. Fluffy crinkled his nose in disgust.

"It stinks down here!" said Abby.

"Yeah, it smells like sewers," Commander You You agreed.

"It looks like it could have been one a long time ago," said Abby.

"It probably was," said Commander You You. "I believe they built this tunnel when they were besieged by Yinksa 10 years ago."

"How did you know that?" Abby asked.

"I taught myself how to read when I was on the Planet Yinksa. One of the guards gave me an entire set of history books about the planet Yinksa, their wars, sieges and conquests of other kingdoms.

They walked down the tunnel until they saw a small pinpoint of light and heard loud voices up ahead.

"We must be near the middle of the town," said Abby.

"Yes, we should probably wait till it gets dark so they will not notice us go by."

"They're all at least 50 feet tall, and it won't be terribly easy for them to see us. But, still, I don't think we really want to get smushed."

"Yes, it would probably be best to wait till its dark," Commander You You agreed.

"We've only one day left to return the Imperial Diamond to King Ufa Gufa," said Abby.

They waited for two long hours until they saw the small beam of light get smaller, and smaller, and smaller until it was all dark. All they could see were the bright stars and the rooftops of several very, very large houses.

"Come on. I think the giants are all asleep by now," said Commander You You.

They quietly climbed out of the tunnel and into the cool night air.

"How do we know where the treasury is?" whispered Commander You You to Abby.

"It's probably in the palace," said Abby. "But, how do we get to the palace? It's like one mile for every step the giants take. How will we get there and find the palace? Let's try that gigantic building over there. It seems like the biggest building there is."

"Well, we can always try it," said Commander You You.

They walked forward until they found a

gigantic tire, thanks to Fluffy's amazing curiosity. He had been wandering close to Commander You You and Abby, but occasionally straying off to look at large toys that had been left outside, rubber left by trucks and truck ships and other things left on the roadside by the giants. When he was exploring he found the tire and meowed as if to let Commander You You and Abby know he had found something useful. They climbed in the middle of the tire putting Fluffy between them. Using their hands and feet, they pushed against the rough insides of the tire. The inside of the tire was enormous. The girls could fit Fluffy between them and still be side by side. They kept rocking it back and forth with their legs until they started moving bit by bit and built up momentum from there. On the downhills they were going about 50 miles an hour with enough momentum to easily glide up the uphills. Before they knew it, they were at the gate of the extremely large mansion.

"There probably is security on this thing," said Abby.

They went along carefully, still in their tire, until suddenly they heard a little click and a whole bunch of gigantic darts came whizzing at them.

"Watch out!" said Abby. "We should have guessed this thing was booby trapped!"

The tire deflated when one of the darts pierced it. They jumped out just before they were squashed by the tire.

Commander You You, Abby and Fluffy quickly lay down on their stomachs and watched as several more gigantic darts flew above them.

"I think we'll have to crawl under them," said Commander You You. "Like on our stomach."

"Yup," said Abby. "Well, it won't hurt to try."

For a while, they slid along their bellies across the dark and mysterious courtyard until finally they realized they had crossed the entire courtyard and were at the door.

"We made it. I think that was all," said Commander You You. "Wait a minute. Why is the door handle blinking?"

"I don't know," said Abby. "But I don't think it's good."

"Me neither," said Commander You You.

Just then there was a little poof and the door handle let out a little bit of white floury powder that made them cough. They realized it was spaceide, which is equivalent to gun powder.

"I think the exploding door handle malfunctioned," said Commander You You hopefully.

"It's never good when anything malfunctions, even if it's something bad," said Abby.

They cautiously opened the door and stepped inside. It was extremely dark and they didn't think anyone lived there until they saw a small, faint beam of light.

"Uh oh, I think one of the giants heard the alarm. Quick! Let's hide behind that gold statue of the 80-foot tall bear," whispered Abby.

They scurried behind the gold statue just as a 50-foot tall man came into the room.

"What was that? If that was HIOC coming back to get my diamond, he will be mashed into a pancake! Well, anyway, I'll sit up here until the morning to see if he shows himself. He can't get to the treasury without passing me. Ha ha ha ha ha," said the giant, yawning.

"Come on," whispered Abby. "Let's try that passageway on the left. Maybe that will lead to the treasury."

They snuck out from behind the statue and slowly crawled across the room. Halfway there, the giant said, "What? Is that another one of those pesky mice? No, it's too small for a mouse. I bet it's that nasty miser HIOC with one of his advisors coming to take back the Imperial Diamond that he so nicely gave me. I will squish him."

"Uh oh! Run! Come on, Abby!"

They reached the corridor, hotly pursued by the giant yelling, "Come back here you diamond stealer, you!"

"Wait," Commander You You said. "We can't outrun him. I have an idea. If we hide by the wall, then he'll pass us without noticing, and we can grab onto him and get a ride. Take Fluffy and put him in my backpack."

"That's a great plan!" Abby agreed.

Accordingly, they hid by the wall and jumped onto the giant's foot when he passed.

"Phew! Does this guy ever take a shower?" said Abby.

"Probably not," said Commander You You.

"Well, anyway, let's get off of this guy as soon as possible."

"Yeah, I don't think he's on his way to the treasury."

They hopped off the giant, which was extremely difficult because they were constantly being lifted high up in the air and then almost smashed down on the ground. But, eventually, they managed to hop off and hide behind a door until he was out of sight.

"We have to find the treasury," said Abby.

"Yes, maybe if we ask the giant in person he might tell us."

"What do you mean ask him in person? He'd squish us!"

"I guess you're right. Maybe we can find it on our own," said Commander You You.

"Wait! Do I hear the clinking of coins?" said Abby.

"I hear it, too!" agreed Commander You You.

"Let's follow the sound and see if that leads us to the treasury."

Chapter 8

Fluffy Plays With Lava

Abby and Commander You You followed the clinking sound for what seemed like hours. All the passages and doors looked exactly the same even though they thought they had walked 10 miles. To the giants, of course, it was like just down the hall.

Gradually, the sound of the clinking coins and voices grew louder until, finally, they saw a light ahead and two shadowy figures talking quietly in the middle of huge heaps of gold, silver, precious metals, diamonds, rubies and every rich thing you could imagine.

"That's a lot of gold," said one of the figures.

"Yes, and it's also *my* gold," the other figure retorted. "If you want any of my gold you'll have to pay for it."

"But I don't have any money to pay for it. And you charge me so much more than it's worth."

"That's the point! You charge more than the gold is worth. You get rich. That's how people make their money."

"Yes, I know that. I just need 10 pieces of gold? Please? Just so I can buy a spaceship and move to Yinksa."

"No! Find yourself a spaceship! I will not give you any money."

"Please, Your Majesty, please. All I need is 10 gold coins."

"I said, no! Now get out of here you filthy peasant scum!"

"Come on," Abby whispered.

"Wait, Abby. It's not all solid ground. Look, there's a little patch of solid ground here and all the rest of it around it is lava."

The lava was orange red and made huge bubbles that popped into yellow liquid that sunk down into the orange mass. The lava was smoking hot and omitted clouds of steam and gas that looked like a huge burning fog.

"No wonder no one can get to the door of the treasury. They can't figure out if they will be roasted or not," said Commander You You hesitantly.

"Well, anyway, we've sort of figured out which pieces of ground are hard and which are not."

"That's a relief. But I'm still going to be very, very careful stepping out on these little patches of ground."

The girls cautiously placed one foot on the solid piece of earth.

"Fluffy! What are you doing?" Commander You You whispered loudly as Fluffy tried to dip his paw into the burning lava.

It was too late. Fluffy dipped his paw into the burning lava, but didn't want to take it out. It didn't seem to be hurting him like burning lava should. Eventually he pulled his paw out, and they saw with astonishment that it was completely unharmed.

"Whoa! Fluffy! How did you do that?"

"Meowwww," was the only reply they got.

"How can you be unharmed? That was

molten, hot, burning lava that you dipped your paw into. Well, Fluffy's non burning thing might be useful to us."

Fluffy swam alongside them in the lava as they crossed the patches of ground. Just then Abby's backpack slipped from her shoulder and slipped into the lava and …pssshhhhh. It was immediately consumed and burned.

"Uh oh! The control panel's in there!" said Abby. "And now we won't have a way to get into the treasury!"

"Oh, yes, we will. Look. You see that? The control panel was destroyed but the key wasn't. I don't think the key can be burned."

"Yeah! That makes total sense. The key is probably made of asteroid metal which can't be burned. Only if you explode it with a moon bomb can you actually destroy it."

"Yes, but I believe there is a moon bomb right next to it!"

"Hey, how did that get there?" said Commander You You. "Abby," she said, "they're everywhere!"

Indeed the moon bombs were all around them, evidently being popped up from somewhere deep under the lava.

"There must be robots or people under there activating the bombs when they hear footsteps. Come on!"

Fluffy swam on to one of the patches of ground and ran.

The girls ran as fast as they could toward the treasury door hoping that they would escape before the bombs exploded. Just as they reached the safety of the door they heard a huge BAM, and, behind them, the key and the entryway to the Imperial Diamond exploded.

Chapter 9

The Imperial Diamond
is Found

"Now, how will we get into the treasury? Our way back is cut off, and we can't open this door by ourselves," said Commander You You.

"No, we can't by ourselves, but he can!" Abby pointed to a giant coming from another hall that they hadn't noticed.

The giant was about three feet shorter than the last giant they had seen. He had on a fluorescent purple shirt with yellow trousers, orange socks and blue shoes. If this giant was trying to be sneaky by making himself look like a clown, he was succeeding admirably.

"Where in the world did he come from?"

"I have no idea. But let's just make sure that he doesn't stomp on us!"

"A wise idea," said Abby.

Commander You You and Abby slipped down by the wall to make sure that the giant did not step on them. He went to the treasury and easily pushed open the door.

"Now I will have the Imperial Diamond all for myself! And when the king, foolish as he is, comes along, he will find out that the Imperial Diamond is gone, and I will be the richest and most powerful person in the universe!" the giant said almost jumping up and down with glee.

Abby and Commander You You exchanged a look that said, "This guy is nuts!"

They quietly followed the giant into the treasury. Once they came into the light, they were astounded to see the heaps of gold, silver, rubies, emeralds and gigantic piles of outrageously large diamonds only found in the center of the largest volcano on Lava Lot, the planet they were now on.

"Whoa! That's a whole lot of money," exclaimed the giant in front of them. "I should take the Imperial Diamond and a few other precious stones with me as a reminder of the greatness of His Majesty."

He began to search for the Imperial Diamond, which the girls knew was somewhere close by.

"I'm not seeing any Imperial Diamond here," said the giant. "Maybe I got the wrong treasury. Maybe it's the fourth treasury instead of the second. I'll check."

The giant turned around, and quickly, and not so quietly, strode out of the room.

Just then Abby and Commander You You saw a small glimmer and a gleam in the distance. They ran toward the light and found an extremely large diamond the size of their heads. It was extremely sparkly and, in the rays of light that hit it, it glinted and gleamed like a rainbow. They could see through it, but at the same time they could see their reflection. It looked very smooth.

"Do you think this is the Imperial Diamond?" said Abby.

"Can't be anything else. Look at the label!"

There was a large gold plaque on the stand just below the Imperial Diamond. The inscription on the plaque read:

IMPERIAL DIAMOND
PROPERTY OF THE KING
DO NOT TOUCH
BOOBY TRAPPED

"Let's try throwing a gold coin at it. Maybe the piece of gold will take care of all the booby traps for us," suggested Abby.

They both picked up gold coins and threw them one after another at the Imperial Diamond. As the first coin touched the Imperial Diamond, a gigantic piece of stone covered in spikes dropped from somewhere in the ceiling. If they had not been several feet away, the stone would have crushed them. Just then, a voice on speaker said, "There are more dangerous booby traps to overcome. The Imperial Diamond is safe to touch, but not to carry away."

"Well, we can try touching it. The recording said it was safe," said Commander You You.

"We can try it, I guess. But I don't really like this."

"We don't really have a choice. We're either getting the Imperial Diamond, or we're not getting it."

"Yeah, I guess you're right."

"Well, let's try it."

They very cautiously touched the Imperial Diamond. Nothing happened. To their surprise it was extremely smooth.

"Let's see if we can very carefully and calmly pick it up and very slowly walk with it to the door and then run with it back to the ship," said Commander You You.

"Sounds like a plan," Abby answered.

Accordingly, Abby and Commander You You very carefully and calmly picked up the Imperial Diamond and very slowly walked with it to the door. When they picked it up it was extremely light. They were quite surprised that the Imperial Diamond was so light.

Just as they were about to leave they heard a voice behind them say very softly, "Going so soon? It would be a shame to leave now. You're so close to getting what you want. But yet you're so far away."

"Excuse me, but we have orders from the king to take the Imperial Diamond to him," said Abby craftily.

"Well then, I am the king. So you may take it to me," the king said with a hint of suspicion in his voice. Then, with great dignity, he strode over to the girls and tried

to yank the Imperial Diamond out of
Commander You You's hands.

"But we have to polish it first," said
Commander You You hurriedly.

"Ah, yes, polish it. Then it will be lovely.
Yes, go on. Meet me in my throne room
when you are finished polishing it so that I
may look upon its greatness," the king said
with a sly smile.

"Yes, Your Majesty," they both said
obediently.

Chapter 10

Commander You You and Abby Meet the Tichywicks and Wackamasaurus

Commander You You and Abby quickly hurried past His Majesty and down the hall. Just as they were about to open the door to what they thought would be the center of the town, Abby said, "Wait a minute. Is the door moving?"

"Yes, it is! I do believe the door is covered in Tichywicks!"

Now a Tichywick is a small animal that is about the size of a mouse. It's furry all over and has a long fluffy tail with a small stinger at the end. Its eyes are usually purple, but sometimes orange. They are very shy creatures, but if you touch them they will usually sting you.

"How will we get through and not get stung? They don't look like very happy Tichywicks. Look! They're growling at us," Abby said.

Fluffy tried to paw at one of the Tichywicks. But when it tried to sting him, he quickly retreated to the safety of Commander You You's backpack. Fluffy decided to content himself with hissing at them from the top of Commander You You's backpack.

"If only we had a piece of pizza. I've heard they go nuts for pizza."

"I have a piece of pepperoni in my pocket," suggested Abby.

"That just might work," said Commander You You.

Abby gave her the small piece of pepperoni, and she called to the Tichywicks. "Hey, Tichywicks! You want this yummy piece of pepperoni? It tastes just like pizza. If you want it, go get it!"

As soon as Commander You You threw the small piece of pepperoni, all the

Tichywicks raced to get to the pepperoni to see who would eat it first.

The girls slowly opened the old creaky door.

"This thing hasn't been opened in years," observed Commander You You.

They cautiously walked down the mildewy passage that looked to them like an old sewer that everyone had forgotten about and no one had bothered to clean up. There was everything you could imagine in this sewer. There were plates, bowls, bathtubs, toilets, old soda cans, new soda cans and fans. They even found an old mustard bottle that still had mustard in it.

"Abby...," Commander You You said in a nervous voice, "Fluffy is no longer following us, and he's nowhere in sight!"

"Where could he have wandered off to?" said Abby.

Just then they saw a little tan tail swishing above an old tomato sauce can.

"Maybe that's Fluffy!" said Commander You You, starting to run over to where they had seen the tail.

When they reached the spot, they found Fluffy happily devouring an old can of huge sardines. Abby and Commander You You both hugged Fluffy tight and then

Commander You You put the cat in her backpack after putting two or three sardines in there for him to munch on.

They had all gone back to walking when Commander You You said in disgust, "Does anyone ever clean this place?"

"Probably not," said Abby. "They probably forgot about it years ago, and then just dumped the stuff they don't want or the stuff that is broken or cracked down here."

"You mean like that?" said Commander You You when a large soda can dropped from a hole in the ceiling.

"Yup. Just like that."

"Look out!" said Commander You You. They jumped aside quickly before a gigantic shower curtain came down from one of the vents above them. "We better get out of here fast, or we'll be smashed under a toilet or something."

They ran at top speed dodging huge pens and pencils, wrappers, clothing and other discarded items.

"Why are there so many things right now dropping down on us?" said Abby loudly over the noise of things falling into the sewer.

"I think it must be garbage day! They put all their trash into a garbage can, and then they empty the garbage can into one of these holes, and everything comes down at once!"

They kept running as fast as they could, avoiding most of the objects that rained down upon them. A few times blankets or shower curtains fell on them. But these did not hurt, just confused them, as they squirmed to get out from under them. Commander You You and Abby finally saw the door on the opposite side; but it, too, was guarded by Tichywicks.

"Quick! See if you can find a piece of pizza in here before we get smashed. I see Tichywicks up ahead!" Abby shouted.

"Over here. I found a piece of one!"

"Good enough."

"Hey, Tichywicks, we've got a nice big piece of pizza over here. You want it?"

Hundreds of little squeaky sounds came from the Tichywicks as they scurried to the huge piece of pizza Commander You You had thrown some distance away. Commander You You and Abby ran quickly toward the door which had so recently been covered in Tichywicks.

Just then the earth beneath their feet began to shake, and, suddenly, a small trap door opened right where they were standing. Fluffy meowed and hissed as he flew out of

Commander You You's backpack as she fell, and they all dropped into the darkness before them. They seemed to keep falling for a long distance until... *Thump!* They hit something squishy which was definitely not the ground. It was a huge pile of Jell-o!

"What is going on?" said Commander You You. "Where are we? And why are we on top of a huge Jell-o sculpture?"

"Well, at least we still have the Imperial Diamond," said Abby. The diamond was bouncing vigorously beside them.

"But how do we get out of this place?" Abby continued. "There's Jell-o as far as the eye can see. The only way out is up on that little ledge. How in the world can we even get up there?"

"We could hoist each other up," said Commander You You.

"We're not tall enough," said Abby. "What if we try jumping on the bouncy Jell-o and see if that propels us high enough to jump onto the small ledge and then climb through the door?"

"That's a great idea!" said Commander You You.

They jumped as high as they could on the Jell-o. They kept jumping and jumping and missing the ledge.

Eventually, Commander You You got one hand on it and managed to pull herself all the way up. Fluffy understood that they had to get onto the ledge and tried jumping as high as he could, but could not reach the ledge until Commander You You grabbed him and lifted him up. He crawled under Commander You You's backpack and looked down at Abby, who was still trying to climb onto the ledge.

"Come on, Abby! I'll get your hand, and then you can get up here," said Commander You You encouragingly.

"I'm trying," said Abby. She jumped as high as she could and caught Commander You You's hand. She handed the Imperial Diamond to Commander You You just before the Jell-o, which they had noticed was gradually getting smaller, disappeared completely underneath them.

Suddenly, something that they hadn't expected and didn't even know still existed came out of where the Jell-o had once stood.

"What in the world is that?" said Commander You You.

It was an animal about the size of a bus with horns like a goat. But its skin was purple with yellow dots all over it. Its eyes were black and beady.

"There's only one thing that could be," said Abby horrified. "The one and only immortal Wackamasaurus!"

Chapter 11

Commander You You and Abby Find Out the Wackamasaurus' Favorite Food

"Hurry! Let's get through that tiny passage before it finds and catches us!" shouted Commander You You.

Abby and Commander You You hurried as fast as they could through the small door they had climbed up to. They ran through it as quickly as they could, only to find another door which was locked.

"Do you have a key?" asked Commander You You.

"Why do you think I would have a key?" said Abby.

"Just checking," Commander You You replied.

They tried pushing on the door, but it would not yield; so they tried to go under the door, but the crack was too small, and they could not make it bigger.

"How will we ever escape? We've got less than 24 hours to get the Imperial Diamond back," said Abby.

"Wait, I hear footsteps. I think someone is coming," said Commander You You.

Just as they were speaking, the door opened and a man stepped through it and went towards the Wackamasaurus. He said to it lovingly, "My pretty little Wackamasaurus, are you hungry? I bet you'd like to have some more Jell-o to eat wouldn't you? You ate all of it. I just gave that to you half an hour ago."

Commander You You and Abby had not noticed a rope dangling from the ceiling. When the giant pulled on the rope, a huge trap door in the ceiling swung open and what Commander You You and Abby thought was 900 pounds of Jell-o dropped into the pit where the Wackamasaurus was roaring. As soon as the Jell-o fell, the

Wackamasaurus pounced upon it and began to eat.

Abby and Commander You You slipped through the door and ran down the passageway the man had come through.

Just then they heard voices up ahead saying, "The Imperial Diamond is missing! Find it! Find it! HIOC has come again and stolen the Imperial Diamond! Find IT! Anyone who can hear me look for it! Find IT! Arrest the traitors!"

Chapter 12

Commander You You and Abby Get Into a Giant Pickle

"Uh oh! They are after us! We are now considered the traitors of HIOC. We need to get out of here right now!" Commander You You shouted.

"But how will we do that with them searching all over the palace for us?"

"I don't know, but we've got to go somewhere. We can't just stay here and let them find us."

They continued to run down the passageway. The voices of the screaming townspeople and guards kept getting louder and louder and louder until they came upon a mob of people shouting around a group of three small figures. One of them they distinctly recognized as HIOC. His HIOC looked bewildered and frightened as he tried to convince the mob that he was someone who just looked like HIOC but wasn't actually him.

"You're HIOC alright! You even have a royal crown and a badge saying that you qualify for how large you are!" said one of the guards in the crowd.

"Well, all right. I am HIOC. But I am greatly, greatly honored to be HIOC. HIOC is the greatest king in the world!"

"Really? I don't think so, buddy. Cause guess what? You're not the one who has the Imperial Diamond. Two kids got it from you. You're just about the lamest king I've ever heard of. You let two little kids steal the most precious piece of treasure and power in the universe. That is so weak. But I guess we'll let you go because you're not a real threat without the Imperial Diamond."

"Oh! I'm the largest threat you have ever heard of!" HIOC bellowed.

"Really? Then why don't you just smash us into the ground, Mr. Big Threat!" said one of the guards who seemed to be an authority.

"I'm feeling gracious today, and I've decided not to. And there is nothing that will make me do it," said HIOC imperiously.

"Really? Nothing in the world?"

"I doubt it."

"Anyhow, be on your way. We have important matters to deal with. So, you, with your pathetic ship can go back to where you came from in peace. And be grateful that we didn't want to steal anything of yours because we easily could have. Now be on your way," said the guard authoritatively.

"You should be grateful that I didn't smash your entire city!" HIOC fumed.

"No, we're not grateful for that. You couldn't even if you wanted to," another guard taunted.

"Well, we'll see about that as soon as I count how many gold coins there are in my treasury. You can do the same, and whoever has the most will get to rule the other country."

"Why would we accept that offer?" said one of the people in the crowd. "We don't want to rule your kingdom of pasta!"

"Perhaps not. So, I'll just come and invade your country after I've had lunch."

"Well, if you insist. We will invade your country as well."

"All right then, it's settled. We will invade each other's countries. This will be fun when you lose and we win!"

"It will be simply fantastic," said one of the officials in the crowd sarcastically.

"Well, now, be on your way," said another of the officials.

"Goodbye, people of Lava Lot. I hope you will welcome me when I march in triumph." The entire crowd booed so loud that HIOC finally got the message that HE SHOULD LEAVE. HIOC waved goodbye and boarded his spaceship, and the crowd dispersed.

Commander You You and Abby quietly went through the streets, unnoticed, because everyone else was so much bigger than they were, and they were so very, very small compared to the giants.

"Hopefully, we should be able to get to our ship," said Abby. "But how do we know where the trap door is?"

"That might be a problem," said Commander You You quietly to Abby. "I'm thinking we should head to the front gate and just walk on out with the rest of the crowd."

"It's worth a try," agreed Abby. "It's got to work with only one day left to get the Imperial Diamond back."

"And if we don't," said Commander You You, "HIOC will find it, and you know whoever has the Imperial Diamond will have the power to rule the galaxy."

"Then why didn't King Ufa Gufa use it?" said Abby.

"Because King Ufa Gufa is a good king, and he doesn't want to rule the galaxy. He wants to see to the welfare of his people. No one wants to attack him because he has the Imperial Diamond, and he could unleash its power and take over anyone. And you know what HIOC would do with it. He would want to rule the entire galaxy."

"Here's a group of people heading toward the gate. We should probably follow them," suggested Abby.

As they were going out, a guard stopped them and said, "Hey! You're too small to be one of our people, and you have the Imperial Diamond! I'm going to arrest you for robbery!"

"Please, sir. We are here on special business for His Majesty to make sure that HIOC does not find the diamond. We're commissioned to hide it in one of the other volcanoes so that when he comes back with his pathetic army, they won't be able to find the Imperial Diamond.

"Well... I suppose. You can't do much harm with the Imperial Diamond. You don't rule a country. You don't even know how the diamond works. So, all right, you may pass."

"Thank you, sir," they said nicely and walked off with the rest of the crowd.

"Apparently, the people of Lava Lot aren't very bright," Abby pointed out. "I suppose they have been living alone so long that they don't know the difference between an enemy and a friend."

"Well, anyway, let's see if we can get out of here and find a ship to take us back to King Ufa Gufa's palace. Only thing is, their spaceships would be way too big for us because they are so much larger than us. We'll have to find our spaceship if we want to get off the planet."

"It would take up to a day to walk all the way around the volcano," said Abby.

"How on earth will we get there fast enough?" asked Commander You You.

"Our time is running out! We can't waste it looking for our spaceship," said Abby.

"Wait a minute! I've heard that on one of

the other volcanoes they keep pet dragons that they use like spaceships," said Commander You You with a hopeful smile.

"Live spaceships? That just doesn't seem right."

"Well, it's worth a shot. We don't exactly have anywhere else to go."

"I think it's that one to the left that has the odd sounds coming from it," suggested Abby, pointing to a large volcano.

"Only one way to find out," said Commander You You.

They started walking. When they got to the volcano, they found a small door guarded by two guards.

"How can we get in there?" Abby wondered.

"I don't know," said Commander You You. "We can't really slip past the guards very easily."

Just then they heard voices and quickly hid behind a large boulder. They saw two giants coming up the path.

"I think I have a plan," said Abby. "If one of us holds Fluffy and the other jumps onto the giant, takes Fluffy and then the other jumps on as well, we'll both be able to get in and get a dragon and get out. How does that sound?"

"That sounds like an excellent plan."

Accordingly, when the giant got closer, Commander You You jumped onto the giant's foot, and before the giant raised his foot again, Abby passed Fluffy over and climbed on beside her friend. They held on to the giant's foot very tightly to make sure that they didn't fall off.

After a while the giant stopped and talked to the guards for a few minutes and went inside the stables where they kept the dragons. Abby and Commander You You hopped off. They stared in awe at the gigantic dragons that were before them.

Most of the dragons were brownish black with white spots that looked like little stars. A couple of them were purple and blue.

The giants bred them so they would blend in nicely with space, and they could sneak up on people or planets and not be seen.

One extremely large dragon was all gold and the front of his stall was silver with gold trimming and a gold name plate that said:

<u>FRED</u>
<u>Property and Royal Steed</u>
<u>of the King</u>

The girls remembered that they had to get a dragon before the officials left. One dragon looked like it would be the perfect one for them. This dragon had no name plate on the front of his stall. He was about the size of a Belgian horse. Unlike all of the other dragons, he was green all over with gold stripes on his wings and silver spines on his back and tail. His tail curved unusually high. Even though his body looked big and fierce, his face was kind and gentle.

As they were looking at the dragon, Fluffy trotted over to the dragon's stall and started looking earnestly at the dragon. The dragon started to move toward Fluffy. When they were just three feet away from each other, the dragon nuzzled Fluffy like a big dog. Fluffy happily danced round and round the dragon. While all this was going on, Abby and Commander You You had been crouched on the floor. They looked at each other, and they both had an idea. Could Fluffy and the dragon somehow know each other?

Abby broke the silence. "I think that this is the dragon for us."

He was smaller than the others, but he looked nice and like he would be able to go very quickly, which was exactly what they needed. Commander You You picked up Fluffy, and they ran toward the dragon and, with some difficulty, mounted on his back.

"How are we going to direct him where to go?" asked Abby.

"Well, maybe we can talk to him, and he will listen to us and move in the direction we want to go," suggested Commander You You.

They tried quietly speaking to the dragon and asking him to move forward, and, to their surprise, he did. They realized, however, that the guards had noticed that a dragon not mounted by an official was moving out of its stall. The guards began to rush forward to stop the dragon Commander You You and Abby were riding. But the small dragon took off in a moment, past the guards, and flew through the air leaving Lava Lot behind them.

"That was close!" said Commander You You.

"I never ever want to go back to Lava Lot again," said Abby.

They told the dragon to go to the planet Linkalonk where King Ufa Gufa was waiting for them to return the Imperial Diamond.

They had been traveling for about an hour when they saw a small dot quickly moving toward them.

"Is that an asteroid or a spaceship?" said Abby. "It's moving too fast for an asteroid. It has to be a spaceship. I really hope that it's not one of HIOC's spaceships or one of the spaceships from the planet Yinksa."

As the ship got closer they realized that it was a ship from HIOC. Looking behind them, the girls saw two dragons with giant riders on them and knew that there would be no escape.

Chapter 13

Albert to the Rescue

"Quick! Where can we hide the diamond?" said Commander You You.

Abby had been hiding it under her clothes to make one of them look very fat, but that wouldn't work anymore because HIOC would probably have them searched when he caught them. They looked frantically around the dragon for anything they might have brought with them in which to hide the Imperial Diamond.

"I don't think we'll be able to hide it," said Commander You You in despair.

"There must be somewhere that we can hide it," said Abby.

The ship was now within 200 yards of them and was closing in fast. They looked to their left, and, to their surprise and dismay, they saw another spaceship closer than the one in front of them. Desperately, they looked to their right to see if there was a way of escape that way. But, again, there was another spaceship.

Then Commander You You had an ingenious idea.

Commander You You suggested they tie the reins, which were quite large and strong, to the feet of their dragon, making a sort of swing seat. Then the girls would climb down into the seat, holding Fluffy in the backpack and the Imperial Diamond in their hands.

They did this, hanging onto the underside of the dragon so that HIOC's ships and the dragons and their riders from Lava Lot couldn't see them from in front or behind or on either side. The girls watched breathlessly as HIOC's ships got closer along with the dragons from Lava Lot.

Finally, HIOC's ships arrived in front of Commander You You and Abby's dragon, and HIOC himself mounted onto the animal. He and some of his soldiers began to search for the Imperial Diamond, Abby and Commander You You and anything else of value.

After about two minutes of searching, the dragons from Lava Lot came up, and the leader dismounted onto the smaller dragon Abby and Commander You You were hiding under. He asked HIOC rather roughly what he was doing there.

"I am looking for two kids who stole the Imperial Diamond from me," said HIOC imperiously.

"Well, that seems rather familiar. They stole the Imperial Diamond from us and took off on one of our dragons, which is right here. We plan to take the Imperial Diamond back with us if we find it," said one of the officials from Lava Lot in an authoritative voice.

"You won't be taking anything back," said another of the officials. "The Imperial Diamond belongs to us now, and you aren't going to get it."

"Oh, yeah. I don't know about that," said HIOC.

Meanwhile on the underside of the dragon, Commander You You and Abby were hanging onto the scales which projected from his belly and listening to the conversation above. They had never been under a dragon before, and they both decided that they weren't going to try it again. The underside of the dragon was a little bit slimy and smelled like fish.

"Abby," Commander You You asked, "When do you think they'll leave? Do you think they'll take the dragon back to Lava Lot? Or do you think HIOC will keep the dragon as one of his fine, collectible items?"

Just then they heard HIOC say, "I believe that since you want the Imperial Diamond, and the Imperial Diamond is obviously not here that I will take this dragon for a nice little display. Don't you think it would look nice in the main hall?" he asked one of his officials.

"Oh, yes, Your Majesty. It would be elegant in the main hall."

"And why do you think that I will let you take one of my prize dragons?" said one of the officials from Lava Lot.

"I don't think you'll let me take it. But because I am king, and ruler, and supreme overlord, as well as being king, tyrant, so on and so forth of the Universe, I can take anything I want."

"Oh, yeah, you think you're the greatest king in the universe? Well, do you have

4,000,922 gold coins in one of your treasuries? That's what we have in one of our treasuries. We have nine treasuries and that's the smallest one," said one of the officials tauntingly.

"Ah, but I have eleven treasuries; so that beats your nine," HIOC retorted.

"However many treasuries you have, we are still the supreme overlords because we are bigger than just about everything."

The officials and HIOC kept fighting for about 10 minutes. Commander You You and Abby felt a sudden movement as HIOC put a rope around the dragon's neck. HIOC tied the rope to the ship and the dragon was obliged to follow as HIOC sped away towards the Pasta Planet.

"What will we do now?" said Abby.

"I don't know," Commander You You admitted. "As soon as they search the dragon they'll find us."

"We have to find a way off of here," Abby persisted.

"Wait! I have an idea," said Commander You You. "What if one of us climbs up onto the neck of the dragon and cuts the rope?"

"That's a fantastic idea!" said Abby.

Abby started to climb from the underbelly of the dragon up to his back. His scales were very smooth, but they were so large that Abby could put her hands around one and pull herself up. It was hard work but after about 10 minutes, she was on the back of the dragon. Abby saw that there was a long pasta-like rope dangling from the dragon's neck. She also noticed a steel chain that was hanging around his neck.

"We just have to make sure that the dragon won't try to run away when we start to cut the rope with the knife," Abby pointed out.

"Let's try talking to the dragon and see if he'll just stay calm."

"But, we don't know its name yet, so how do we address it?" asked Abby.

"Wait a second! Is that a name plate?" said Abby in surprise, looking down at the round disk of bronze hanging on the steel chain around the dragon's neck.

"I think it is," agreed Commander You You craning her neck forward until she could see the edge of the name plate.

"Let's see what the name plate says, and that must be the dragon's name," said Abby hanging on to one of the silver spikes on the dragon's neck and trying to grab the chain. She caught the chain in her hand, and, still hanging on to the spike, put her feet on the top of the name plate. Looking down on it, she was able to make out the words. Abby read the name plate out loud. It said:

ALBERT
Royal Possession of the King of Lava Lot and Ruler of all Giants In the Universe

"Well, it's good that we know his name," said Commander You You. "Let's try and see if he'll allow us to cut the rope."

Abby climbed back up the chain and pulled herself onto the dragon's back.

"Albert," Abby said quietly, "please let us cut the rope so that we can get out of here, and then you can come live with us instead of going back to Lava Lot."

Albert made a little grunting noise that they both thought might be yes. Quietly, Abby began to cut the rope which unsurprisingly was made of pasta. But this pasta was very strong and wouldn't break easily.

While Abby was cutting the rope, HIOC was staring out of the front windshield of his spaceship and eating out of a huge bowl of ketchup and papaya. Abby worked about five minutes on cutting the rope when there was a little *snap* and the pasta rope broke.

Commander You You lifted up Fluffy who quickly scrambled onto Albert's back. Abby held out her hand to take the Imperial Diamond while Commander You You climbed up to join them. When they were both securely on top of Albert's back they flicked the reins a little bit, and Commander You You said, "Go to the planet Linkalonk and King Ufa Gufa's palace."

But just at that moment, HIOC noticed that the dragon was no longer following a straight course behind his ship.

"Uh oh, do you think HIOC has noticed something?" said Abby in a worried tone.

"I'd say he's found out," said Commander You You. They looked to the right to where HIOC's ship was and saw HIOC staring out of a window. He appeared to be screaming something that was probably an insult or a curse.

Albert flew at top speed toward the planet Linkalonk. Evidently, he knew the way perfectly. But HIOC would not give up. He was trying his best to catch the dragon before he got anywhere close to the planet of

Linkalonk. After about an hour of flight, Linkalonk came into view; but HIOC was close behind, and the dragon, Albert, was starting to get weary of flying so fast. Abby and Commander You You knew they could not outrun HIOC, and they didn't see how they could get to Linkalonk before HIOC caught them.

Just then, the girls saw three dragons coming into view behind HIOC's ship and realized that the men from Lava Lot weren't happy about HIOC taking one of their dragons as a prize. HIOC had just finished his bowl of ketchup and papaya and was now shouting orders and cursing that no one was getting him more ketchup and papaya. The captain of the ship was also shouting, trying to tell him something. But HIOC was so outraged at the lack of ketchup and papaya that he would not listen to the captain who was telling them that they were being followed.

Just as Commander You You and Abby were about to get captured by HIOC, HIOC finally noticed that giants were following them. He ordered his soldiers to load the guns. Unfortunately, when he decided to fire the guns, the guns only fired ketchup-covered papaya pieces at the dragons. The guns did no harm except for turning some of the giants and dragons a slightly red color.

"Oh, so that's where I stored the extra food for His Majesty," said the steward in a composed tone of voice.

"Why didn't you store it in the barrels?" bellowed HIOC angrily.

"All the barrels were filled with gnoccis!" (Gnoccis, a French food made out of potatoes, were the substitute for cannon balls on the Pasta Planet.)

Before HIOC could rant further, there was an enormous roar from outside, and the dragons overtook them.

"What's this?" HIOC roared.

"It seems to be an attack by Lava Lot!" said one of his officers.

"I know it's an attack from Lava Lot!" HIOC fumed. "Who else would have the nerve to attack me?"

The dragons carrying their enormous riders started to batter HIOC's ship. Since they were apparently war dragons due to their bulk and size, the ship kept turning from right to left, left to right, over and over until finally Abby and Commander You You saw HIOC's ship turn and fly at top speed back to the Pasta Planet.

But Abby and Commander You You

weren't safe yet. They'd only exchanged one enemy for another. The dragons from Lava Lot were quickly coming up behind them, and they weren't on a friendly visit. Commander You You and Abby could see the dragons not far behind. The dragons roared in back of them, and when they let out their breath they smelled strongly of sulfur.

"Come on!" said Commander You You desperately. "We have to get to King Ufa Gufa's palace before the dragons catch us!"

Albert understood that if they didn't get away he would have to go back to a boring stall and have a fat official riding on his back. He flew as fast as he could straight for the doors of King Ufa Gufa's palace. The big dragons were now only 20 feet behind them, and the girls knew that if they did not hurry they would be back on Lava Lot as prisoners.

Fluffy meowed loudly, pointing one paw to the foremost of the dragons following them and looking at Albert meaningfully. Albert grunted several times, and it was clear to the girls they were having a deep conversation. A couple moments later, Albert put on a burst of speed that left the Lava Lot dragons far behind. They burst through the doors of the palace and skidded into one of the halls. They narrowly missed hitting King Ufa Gufa in the face with one of Albert's legs as he ran out to see what all the commotion was about.

"What's going on? And why did you bring this thing into my palace?" said King Ufa Gufa, pointing at Albert.

"Your Majesty, we have brought back the Imperial Diamond in the time that you promised," said Commander You You.

"Impossible! No one can get the Imperial Diamond except for ummmmm????" He turned to one of his officials and said, "Who can get the Imperial Diamond from HIOC?"

"Apparently, they can, sir," said the official. "Look! They're carrying the Imperial Diamond."

"Why, that is my Imperial Diamond!" The king snatched it from Commander You You. "I have missed the Imperial Diamond so very, very much," he said, hugging it like it was alive. "Thank you for returning the most precious Imperial Diamond to my palace."

"You're quite welcome, Your Majesty," said Commander You You and Abby respectfully. "But now, if you don't mind I think we'll be heading home. The monkeys have probably raided the entire pantry," said Commander You You laughing.

"Probably raided the entire pantry? Absolutely they raided the entire pantry," said Abby.

They mounted Albert and started on the journey back to their island, back to the quiet life they had led before the Imperial Diamond was stolen.

Epilogue

The Disappearance

When Commander You You and Abby
got home, they saw that the animals had
pretty much made a mess of everything.
After a few days it was all cleaned up.
Commander You You and Abby built Albert
a sort of stable with a comfy pile of straw
and a heaping trough full of his new favorite
food, pineapple. He became great friends
with the other animals, especially Fluffy
who spent most of the day around Albert.
He was even friends with the python,
Hercules, who usually put his head under his

coils and wouldn't look up or be sociable with anyone but Commander You You and Abby.

During the day, Albert and some of the other animals went with Commander You You and Abby to run errands, do chores or just have a great time. Albert settled into the quiet life full of fun and joy that Commander You You and Abby had led before, when they were just two little kids on an island in space.

They never used their old spaceship that the kind man had given them and wondered if he would ever come back so they could give him his ship. Occasionally, he sent them letters by the Galatic Post with no return address. Abby and Commander You You thought this was a little odd, but his letters were always interesting. They told about places he had gone, adventures he had had and interesting information he had found and sometimes included pictures that he had collected from all different parts of the galaxy.

This went on for about three months until a messenger sent by King Ufa Gufa arrived. All of the people on King Ufa Gufa's planet regarded the girls as heroes and paid them the utmost respect. The messenger gave them the message, bowing deeply as he did so. The message was that a force was ready to attack the Pasta Planet, and they would like Commander You You and Abby to be there when they conquered the planet and made HIOC a shameful prisoner.

Somewhat reluctantly the girls agreed, and, mounting on their beloved friend, Albert, they quickly arrived at the gates of the palace of King Ufa Gufa. There they saw a magnificent force of all of the men in the army on Linkalonk. All of the men were angry and shouting, wanting to be the first to cut down a pasta person.

King Ufa Gufa made a very boring speech that Abby and Commander You You didn't listen to at all. Then the force started for the Pasta Planet in spaceships or whatever mode of transportation they had. Leading the way, Abby and Commander You You went to attack the Pasta Planet. But when they got to the place where the planet had always been, there was no planet in sight.

"What's going on?" everyone shouted. "Have you led us to the wrong spot?" a few of them said.

"No, the Pasta Planet was definitely here. It's my personal theory that the planet has disappeared," announced King Ufa Gufa.

Everyone began to talk to his neighbor and wonder. Where had the planet gone? And how had it magically disappeared?

"Abby," said Commander You You, "I don't know how HIOC and his entire planet disappeared, but if he does come back he will come with a large force for revenge. And he'll either show up by our island or by Linkalonk. He knows we wouldn't stand a chance, so he'll probably hit us first."

"You're right," agreed Abby. "But we don't have anything we can fight him with. I guess we'll just have to be alert for when he does come."

"Exactly," said Commander You You. "If we're alert and we know when he returns, we can go for help."

While they'd been talking this over, King Ufa Gufa gave a long speech and told them that HIOC would probably soon return, and they would be able to take him captive in perhaps two weeks. After this, the force dispersed and went to their different homes. Abby and Commander You You, with Albert, went back to the quiet life they had led before HIOC had stolen the Imperial Diamond.

Once Commander You You and Abby arrived home, they decided to talk over how they might prepare for when HIOC would come back. If he could choose where to go, he would probably go right to King Ufa Gufa to get the Imperial Diamond and then go to their planet. The girls decided they would train some of their animals to keep watch around the island to see if they noticed any signs of the planet returning. If they saw the planet returning, the animals would make a certain signal, and then the girls would know that the planet was coming back and be able to get King Ufa Gufa's army to help them.

A month later, one of the animals on watch gave the signal that said there was something odd going on. Commander You You and Abby came over to the spot where the animal was frantically jumping up and down and pointing at weird flashes that repeated themselves in the sky. The flashes were almost like lightning except far, far out in space. They were coming from the direction of the Pasta Planet and were just tiny flashes. The girls knew that one day soon HIOC would return.

The End

Acknowledgments

I would like to thank my writing teacher, Miss Ann, for inspiring me to write this book and helping me edit. I'd like to thank my mom who typed this story for over six months through lots of revisions. I also would like to thank my dad for getting me thinking about the world that my characters live in through a funny game we used to play. I really would like to thank Miss Ann's writing group for giving me fantastic feedback and encouraging me. Thank you so much, Abby, for being a fantastic inspiration and a great friend. Thank you, David, for just being David and giving me an idea for my sequel. I would really, really like to super thank Sydney who helped a lot through the process of this story and was also in my writing class. Thank you, Miss Jo, for helping me with my cover art. I don't think I could have come up with it without you. Last, but not least, I'd like to thank my cat, Fluffy, for giving me an idea for the super space cat in my story. You really are quite an amazing cat!

About the Author

Commander You You and the Imperial Diamond is Lauren-Kate Stewart's first novel. She is 10 years old, homeschooled and lives in North Carolina with her parents and pets. Lauren-Kate likes animals and mythology. Her favorite subject is history. She has a cat named Fluffy, who was the inspiration for the cat in the story.

THE BRIDGE

A medium that transports
story from inspiration to creation.
Our desire is that authors and readers
will be affirmed through
creativity and the written word.